THIS LITTLE TIGER BOOK BELONGS TO:

_____

_____

_____

_____

For Eleanor Troth &
Emily Peopall
~ *J.S.*

For Jane,
who *loves* Christmas!
~ *T.W.*

LITTLE TIGER PRESS
An imprint of Magi Publications
22 Manchester Street, London W1M 5PG
First published in Great Britain 1998
This paperback edition published 1998
Text © 1998 Julie Sykes
Illustrations © 1998 Tim Warnes
Julie Sykes and Tim Warnes have asserted their rights
to be identified as the author and illustrator of this work
under the Copyright, Designs and Patents Act, 1988.
Printed in Belgium by Proost NV, Turnhout
ISBN 1 85430 461 5

5 7 9 10 8 6 4

LITTLE TIGER PRESS

London

Hurry, Santa!

by Julie Sykes

illustrated by Tim Warnes

It was Christmas Eve, and Santa's busiest
time of year.

"ZZZzzz," he snored from under his duvet.

"Wake up!" squeaked Santa's little mouse,
tugging at his beard. "Hurry, Santa! You
mustn't be late tonight."

"Ouch!" cried Santa, sitting up and rubbing
his chin. "Goodness, is that the time?
My alarm clock didn't go off and
I've overslept."

Santa leapt out of bed and began to pull
on his clothes. He was in such a hurry that
he put both feet down one trouser leg and
fell flat on his face.

"Hurry, Santa!" mieowed his cat. "You mustn't be late tonight."

"No, I mustn't," agreed Santa, struggling up. "I mustn't be late delivering the presents."

When he was dressed Santa hurried outside to his
sleigh. He picked up the harness and tried to put
it on the reindeer.
But the reindeer weren't there!
"Oh no!" cried Santa. "Wherever have they gone?"

"The reindeer are loose in the woods. You'd better catch them before they wander off," called Fox. "Hurry, Santa, you mustn't be late tonight."

"No, I mustn't," agreed Santa, running towards the trees.

Deep in the woods the reindeer
were having a snowball fight.
"Aaaaah!" cried Santa loudly,
as a snowball hit him in the face.

"Hurry, Santa," hooted Owl. "You haven't got time to play in the snow. You mustn't be late tonight."

"I wasn't playing!" said Santa indignantly. "Come on, you naughty reindeer, we've got work to do."

At last Santa was ready to leave. With a crack
of his whip and a jingle of bells he steered the
sleigh towards the moon.
"Go, Reindeer, go!" he shouted. "We mustn't
be late tonight."

Around the world they flew, delivering presents
to every child.
"Down again," called Santa, turning the sleigh
towards a farm.
"Hurry, Santa!" answered the reindeer. "We're
miles from anywhere, and the night's nearly over."
"I'm doing my best," said Santa, flicking the reins.

Before Santa could stop them the reindeer
quickened their pace.
"Whoa," Santa cried, but it was too late.
Landing with a bump, the sleigh skidded
crazily across the snow.
"Ooooh deeeaaar!" cried Santa in alarm.

CRASH!
The sleigh came to rest in a ditch.
Santa scrambled to his feet and rubbed
his bruised bottom. "Nothing broken,"
he boomed. "But we must hurry!"

When the reindeer had untangled themselves
everyone tried to dig out the sleigh. They tugged
and they pulled and they pushed as hard as they
could, but it was completely stuck.

"It's no good," wailed the reindeer. "We can't move this sleigh on our own."

"We must keep trying," said Santa. "The sky is getting lighter and we're running out of time."

Just then a loud neigh made Santa jump in surprise.
Trotting towards him was a very large horse.
"Hurry, Santa!" she neighed. "You've still not
finished your rounds. *I'll* help you move your sleigh."
Everyone pulled together, even Santa's little mouse,
but it was no good. The sleigh was still stuck.

"Hurry, Santa!" called the cockerel from the gate.
"You must be quick. It's nearly morning."
"I am *trying* to hurry," puffed Santa. "I must deliver
the last of the presents on time."
Then suddenly the sleigh began to move . . .

. . . and Santa shot backwards,
cheering loudly.
"Hurry, Santa!" called all the animals.
"The sun's rising. You must be on your
way before the children wake up."

"Yes, I must," agreed Santa. "It's nearly Christmas Day!"

It was a close thing, but by dawn Santa
had managed to deliver every present.
"We did it!" yawned Santa. "I wasn't . . ."

Santa stopped talking and stared at his sack in dismay. At the very bottom there was still one present left. "Oh no, how awful!" he cried. "I've forgotten someone!"

Then Santa noticed that the animals were laughing.
"That present is for _you_. It's from all of us," said the reindeer.

"Hurry, Santa!" added Santa's little mouse.
"You must open your present. It's Christmas Day!"
"Yes, I must," chuckled Santa. "Now, I wonder
what it is . . ."

Join the
LITTLE TIGER CLUB
now for lots more
books to enjoy!

Schools can
join too and will
receive a special
enrolment pack.

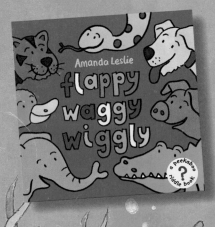

*Join the LITTLE TIGER CLUB now and receive a special Little Tiger goody bag containing
badges, pencils and more! Once you become a member you will be sent details of
special offers, competitions and news of new books. Why not write a book review?
The best reviews will be published on book covers or in the Little Tiger Press catalogue.*

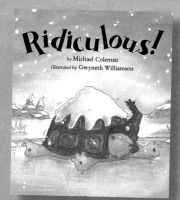

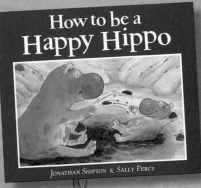

The LITTLE TIGER CLUB is free to join. Members can cancel their membership at any
time, and are under no obligation to purchase any books. If you would like details
of the Little Tiger Club, please contact: Little Tiger Press, 22 Manchester Street,
London W1M 5PG, UK. Telephone: 0171 486 0925, Fax: 0171 486 0926
Visit our website at: www.littletiger.okukbooks.com